# Dedication

I dedicate this to Ky'zah, Brennen, Auden, and Breon. I chose to live life in its full entirety because of you. My sincerest prayer is that I may be a positive example you can learn from, a mother you can be proud of, and the most admirable woman you'll ever know. I love you always and forever.

MOMMA

Here I stand, from the bayous of Louisiana, the first woman in the United States to become a self-made millionaire.  Me! Madam C.J. Walker.

# Louisiana Belle

## A snippet of the life of Madam CJ Walker

Author : LaChanda Casteal

Illustrator : M. Ridho Mentarie

What is a millionaire you ask?  A millionaire is a person who has a lot of money.

Money is not everything, but it can be helpful if put to good use.

With money, you can buy groceries for your family, a house and a new car. You can even buy brand new toys to play with!

There are many ways to make money, but let me tell you how I did it.

9

Everyone would always tell me how they absolutely loved my hair.

They said it always looked so shiny, rich, and healthy.

The compliments I received about my natural hair styles made me feel like the most beautiful girl in the world.

I wanted to make every girl across the world love their hair as much as I loved mine. That is when I came up with an idea!

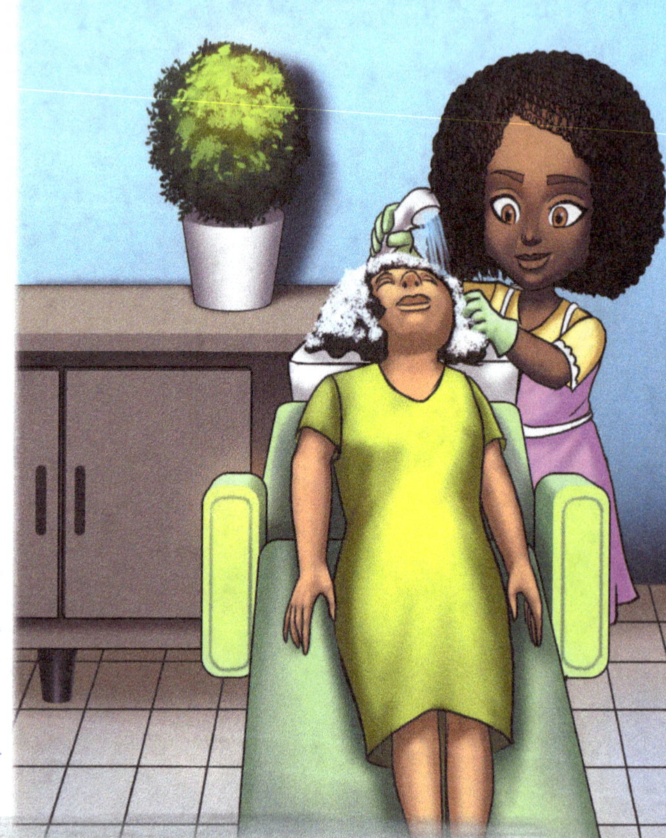

I created shampoos and pomades that helped make people's hair stronger, softer and shinier.

Some people think I created the perm which straightens hair, but that is not true.

15

Actually, because I was in love with my natural hair so much, I created products for others to make their natural hair as fabulous as mine.

And just like magic, my company took off like a rocket! I became a very successful person.

I went from making a dollar a day as a washer woman to being a millionaire.  I learned hard work always pays off.

Even through all of my success I never forgot where I came from. I went out of my way to give back to people who needed help the most.

I gave money to help support my friend Booker's school in Tuskegee.

I gave money for scholarships so less fortunate people could have a chance to go to school.

I also gave to clubs that helped to create better lives for other women and those in less privileged communities as well.

Whatever you decide to do with your life, do it to your best ability.

Love yourself just as you are, because you are beautiful and capable of doing amazing things.

And never forget, as you are blessed with success… bless others as you progress.

www.ingramcontent.com/pod-product-compliance
Lightning Source LLC
Chambersburg PA
CBHW082147130726
47910CB00014B/2613